All the happenings in the Policeman Pete books are
based on true occurrences from the villages of Saddleworth,
a civil parish made up of 7 villages that nestle within the
foothills of the Pennines. These stories have been collected
and re-told by the author, Barbara Ann.

First published in 2013 by Creative Locations Ltd.
Lake House
Brimmycroft
Rochdale Road
Denshaw
Saddleworth
OL3 5UE

E-mail: creativelocations@hotmail.co.uk

Author and Illustrator: Barbara Ann
Graphic Editor: Adelina Pintea

For each book sold, a donation will be made by Creative Locations Ltd.
Every donation will go to a charity called 'The Blue Lamp Foundation' set
up in 2010 by the late P.C.David Rathband, charity number 1138319.
This charity gives financial support to all 999 emergency personnel who
become injured in the line of duty.

The Story of Policeman Pete and The Jumping Frog

by
Barbara Ann
∞
Creative Locations Ltd.

Mr. and Mrs. Pollitt lived in a cottage by the school playing field. They had twins, Harry and Emily.

One day, after it had been raining heavily for over a week, the wall of Mr. and Mrs. Pollitt's garden fell down into the road.

Mr. Pollitt rang Policeman Pete to see what he could do.

'Don't worry,' said Policeman Pete as he looked at the fallen wall. 'I will ring Farmer Bill and ask if Lee, his nephew, could come down with his digger to bucket up the stones to one side, ready for rebuilding.'

4

Once Lee had cleared away the stones from the footpath and road, he discovered that there was an old spring that ran under the wall and into the field at the side of the house.

Harry and Emily Pollitt found all this excitement wonderful. Harry put on his Wellington boots and started to paddle and splash around in the swollen spring water.

Policeman Pete called up to see if the road was clear and laughed at Harry playing in the water.

Just then Harry gave a large squeal.
'Eeeeeek!' he cried and quickly kicked off
his boot.

Emily thought he was doing a Red Indian
war dance.

'Oh dear, I see what the problem is,' said Policeman Pete trying not to laugh.

As he turned Harry's Wellington boot upside-down, a big green frog jumped out!

'Policeman Pete, please catch the frog for me, I would love to hold it!' squealed Emily.

It was easy for Policeman Pete to catch the frog in his big strong hands, but when Emily tried to hold it, her hands were too small and it jumped back into the grass.

Emily and Policeman Pete laughed at Harry. His face was still bright red.

'Urgh,' said Harry, 'The frog was so slimy in my Wellington boot. I don't think I like frogs!'

'Well, I like frogs,' said Emily. 'I am going to call this one Zippo and I will come and see him every day.'

True to her word, Emily checked on Zippo every day to make sure he was not in the road or on the footpath. Emily didn't want Zippo to be squashed by cars or walkers.

As Policeman Pete sat down that evening in front of his fire he had a little chuckle to himself when he thought of Harry and the frog in his Wellington boot.

Another job well done!